WORKING THE FARM

by Mara Conlon
Illustrated by Jesus Redondo

Published by Scholastic Inc., 557 Broadway, New York, NY 10012. SCHOLASTIC and associated logos are trademarks and/or registered trademarks of Scholastic Inc.

ISBN 978-0-545-5

12 11 10 9 8 7 6 5 4 3 2
Printed in the U.S.A.
First printing, Septe

D0967801

SCHOLASTIC INC.

A  is a busy place for trucks.

A uses trucks to help him grow

crops like  ,  , and  vines.

This is bringing beehives to the orchard. The bees carry pollen to the on the . This helps the grow.

When the are ripe, the goes to work. The picks the off the . He puts them in . The will carry the to a cooler for storage.

A also does a lot of work on a . In the spring, the uses a powerful to plant different kinds of . The pulls a row planter through the fields. The row planter drops into the soil.

The  grow into tall stalks of

. Then the uses a

to cut and gather the . The

removes the husks from the ears of

. Harvesting is a big job, and

the does important work

on a .

Trucks do a lot of different jobs

on a . This is so large,

the can't lift it! Instead, he uses

a to pick up the giant

and move it across the .

The trucks on this also help

the care for his animals. The ,

, and on the eat

. This big forage harvester

chops into small pieces.

The is turned into for

the animals to eat.

A  squeezes the together

to form stacks or bales. bales

can be round or square. Then a

 picks up the stacks of

and carries them to the .

Today, the is getting ready for some special visitors. He and the trucks are working very hard to make the look great! The uses a to cut the . He washes the and cleans all of the machines.

Finally, a arrives with the

special visitors. The children are here

to pick . Each child gets a

to load up with tasty .

Now it is time for the ride!

The drives through the fields

of to a patch. Each

child can take home a .

Everyone has had a great day

at the  !

Did you spot all the picture clues in this book?

Each picture clue is on a flash card. Ask a grown-up to cut out the flash cards. Then try reading the words on the backs of the cards. The pictures will be your clues.

Reading is fun with Tonka!

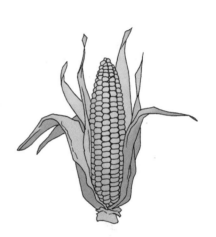

farmer	farm
corn	apples
pickup truck	pumpkin

trees	flowers
crates	flatbed truck
seeds	tractor

forklift	combine harvester
pigs	cow
hay	chicken

baler truck	grass
lawn mower	barn
basket	school bus